Cuddle Up Tight

RED FOX

A Red Fox Book

Published by Random House Children's Books
20 Vauxhall Bridge Road, London SW1V 2SA

A division of The Random House Group Ltd
London Melbourne Sydney Auckland Johannesburg
and agencies throughout the world

3 5 7 9 10 8 6 4 2

First published in the United Kingdom
by the Bodley Head Children's Books 1999

Red Fox edition 2000

Printed in Singapore by Tien Wah Press (PTE) Ltd

THE RANDOM HOUSE GROUP Limited Reg. No. 954009

www.randomhouse.co.uk

ISBN 0 09 941148 2

CONTENTS

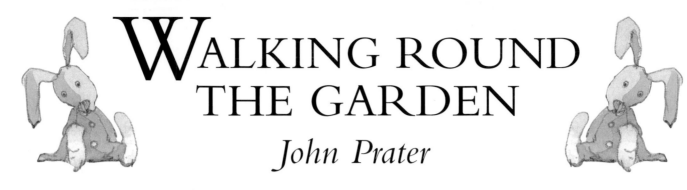

WALKING ROUND THE GARDEN

John Prater

Walking round the garden, like a teddy bear,

One step, two steps, tickle you under there.

Walking down the hallway, up and up the stairs,

One step, two steps, what a clever bear!

Sitting in the bedroom,

What a sleepy ted,

All I need is a goodnight kiss,

Then tuck you into bed.

AN EVENING AT ALFIE'S

Shirley Hughes

One cold, winter evening, Alfie and his little sister, Annie Rose, were all ready for bed. Mum and Dad were all ready to go out, and Mrs MacNally's Maureen was in the living-room. She had come to look after Alfie and Annie Rose while Mum and Dad went to a party.

Alfie and Maureen waved
good-bye to them from
the window.
    Annie Rose was
already in her cot.
Soon she settled
down and went to sleep.

Alfie liked Maureen. She always read him a story when
she came to baby-sit.

Tonight Alfie wanted the story about Noah and his Ark full of
animals. Alfie liked to hear how the rain came drip, drip, drip, and
then splash! splash! splash! and then rushing everywhere, until the
whole world was covered with water.

When Maureen had finished the story it was time for Alfie to
go to bed. She came upstairs to tuck him up.

They had to be very quiet and talk in whispers in case they woke up Annie Rose.

Maureen gave Alfie a good-night hug and went off downstairs, leaving the door a little bit open.

Alfie didn't feel sleepy. He lay in bed
looking at the patch of light on the ceiling.

For a long time all was quiet.
Then he heard a funny noise
outside on the landing.
  Alfie sat up. The noise was
just outside his door. Drip,
drip, drip! Soon it got quicker.
It changed to drip-drip,
drip-drip, drip-drip! It was
getting louder too.

Alfie got out of bed and peeped round the door. There was a puddle on the floor. He looked up. Water was splashing into the puddle from the ceiling, drip-drip, drip-drip, drip-drip! It was raining inside the house!

Alfie went downstairs. Maureen was doing her homework in front of the television.

"It's raining on the landing," Alfie told her.

Alfie and Maureen went back upstairs. The puddle was getting bigger. The drip-drip, drip-drip, drip-drip had turned into a splash! splash! splash!

"Hmm, looks like a burst pipe," said Maureen. A plumber was one of the things she wanted to be when she left school.

"Better get a bucket," she said. So Alfie showed her where the bucket was kept, in the kitchen cupboard with the brushes and brooms.

But now the water was dripping down in another place.

Alfie and Maureen found two of Mum's big mixing bowls and put them underneath the drips.

Maureen got on the telephone to her Mum. The MacNallys lived just across the street.

Mrs MacNally was there in a moment.

"Oh dear, oh dear, it's ruining your mother's floor!" cried Mrs MacNally. "Fetch some floor-cloths, Maureen!"

Just then Annie Rose woke up and began to cry.

"Shh, shh, there, there," said Mrs MacNally, bending over her cot. But Annie Rose only looked at her and cried louder.

Mrs MacNally ran back out to the landing. She and Maureen tried to mop up the water. But now the drips were coming from lots of different places, splash, splash, splash!

"We ought to turn the water off from the main," said Maureen, "but I don't know how you do it. I think I'd better fetch Dad."

While she was gone Mrs MacNally mopped and mopped, and emptied brimming bowls, and in between mopping and emptying she ran to try to comfort Annie Rose. But Annie Rose went on crying and crying. The drips on the landing came faster and faster.

Now there were a lot of puddles on the floor. Alfie paddled in them for a while. It was quite fun but the water was very cold. He thought that soon perhaps the whole street would be covered with water and they would all have to float away in a boat, like Noah's Ark.

Soon Maureen came running upstairs with Mr MacNally close behind her, wearing his bedroom slippers.

"What's all this, then?" said Mr MacNally, looking at all the water pouring down.

He put his head round the bedroom door. He and Annie Rose were old friends.

"Dear, dear, what's all this?" he said in a very kind voice.

Then he went downstairs and found a large sort of tap under the stairs and turned it off, just like that.

"So *that's* where it was," said Maureen.

Then the water stopped pouring down through the ceiling, splash! splash! splash! and became a drip-drip, drip-drip, drip-drip, and then a drip... drip.... drip..... drip...... and then it stopped altogether.

"Oh, thank goodness for that!" said Mrs MacNally.

"I'll know how to do it next time," said Maureen.

But Annie Rose was still crying.

"Don't cry, Annie Rose," said Alfie. And he put
his hand through the bars of her cot and patted her very gently,
as he had seen Mum do sometimes.

Annie Rose still wore nappies at night.

"Annie Rose is wet," Alfie told everyone. "And her bed's wet too.
I expect that's why she's crying."

"Why, so she is, poor little mite!" said Mrs MacNally.

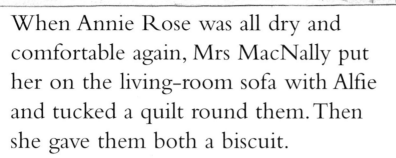

When Annie Rose was all dry and comfortable again, Mrs MacNally put her on the living-room sofa with Alfie and tucked a quilt round them. Then she gave them both a biscuit.

Annie Rose was quite cheerful now. She got very friendly with Mr MacNally and he let her play a game with him, taking off his glasses and putting them on again.

Then she sucked her thumb and leaned up against Alfie, and Alfie leaned up against her. When Mum and Dad came home, they were both fast asleep.

Next morning Mum told Alfie not to turn on the taps until the plumber had been to mend the burst pipe.

Alfie didn't mind not having a wash. He'd had enough water the evening before to last for a long time.

TOO MANY TEDDIES
Gus Clarke

"Mum," said Frank. "There are just too many teddies."
"Nonsense," said Mum. "You can never have too many teddies."

But Frank did.

It started the day he was born.
"A boy needs a bear," said Uncle
Jim. And that was the first...

of many.

He'd get them for birthdays
and for Christmas...

for all sorts of special
occasions...

and sometimes for
no particular reason at all.

By the time he was four there
was more than a bed full.
There were teddies everywhere.

And even the teddies had teddies.

At bedtime his dad would tuck them all in and together they would say goodnight to them. One by one.

It seemed to Frank that if he got many more teddies, by the time they'd said goodnight to them all it would be time to get up!

It was then that Frank knew he'd really got a problem. But the more he thought about it, the more he could see that the problem was not the teddies...

the problem was Dad... and Mum...

...and all the aunties and uncles,
the grandmas and grandpas,
the cousins, the friends and
the neighbours that kept on
giving him all these teddies.

He knew that they all liked
teddies and he knew that they
all liked choosing the teddies.
They'd told him.

They'd spend ages choosing the
cuddliest one, or the cutest one,
the furriest or the funniest one,
the one with the special smile...

or even just the one with
the squeakiest tummy.

In fact, just the sort of teddy that they would like for themselves. But, of course, being so grown up they thought they couldn't really buy it for themselves.
So they bought it for Frank.
At least they could have a little cuddle before they gave it to him.

And that was when he had his idea. Perhaps, thought Frank, if they all had a teddy of their own to cuddle, they wouldn't need to buy quite so many for him.

"Grandma," said Frank. "Would you like to look after my teddy for a little while? I've got plenty more."
And, of course, Grandma was only too pleased.

And so was Aunty Vicky...

and Uncle Roger...

and Cousin Percy...

and the man next door but one.
And everyone else.

Of course, Frank kept one or two for himself – his favourites, and one or two more to keep them company.

And that was that.
They all lived happily ever after. Until one day...

"A boy needs a dog," said Uncle Jim.   And that...

32

...was the first of many.

NEARLY BUT NOT QUITE

Paul Rogers and John Prater

Simon was going to play at James' and Harriet's house for the day.
"Now, be a big boy," said Mum.
But Simon didn't feel very big.
And he didn't wave goodbye
when she went, either.
He stood at the bottom of
the garden steps and looked
around him at the big house,
the big lawn and the great
big trees.

34

"Come on," said James, "let's play Robin Hood." "This can be the camp," said Harriet. "Can you climb up?"

"Nearly," said Simon...

"...but not quite."

"We'll get the supper ready.
You keep a look out,"
said James.
"Can you see over the top?"
said Harriet.

"Nearly," said Simon...

"...but not quite."

"Quick!" said James,
"the sheriff's men
are coming! We're
under attack!"

"Can you fire
a bow and
arrow?"
said Harriet.

"Nearly,"
said Simon...

"...but not quite."

"Look! They're giving themselves up!" said James. "They're waving a white flag!"
"Where?" said Simon. "I can't see it."

"Give me your t-shirt," said Harriet. "But you mustn't tell."
"Big boys don't tell," said James.

"Watch out! It's a trap!"
said James.
"We'll have to escape by
the secret passage. There's
no time to lose."
"Wait for me!" said Simon.

"Where have you
been?" said James.
"Did you get caught?"
"Nearly," said Simon...

"...but not quite."

"They're still behind us!" said Harriet. "There's only one thing for it! We must take the horses."

"Here's yours," said James. "Do you know how to ride?"

"Nearly," said Simon...

"...but not quite."

"They're following our tracks," said James. "Leave the horses here. We'll cross the river."

"Can you step over?" said Harriet.

"Nearly," said Simon...

41

"... but not quite."

"James? Harriet?" called a voice.
"Simon, your mum's here!"
James and Harriet looked at Simon.

Then they looked at each
other. "I want Mummy,"
said Simon.

"What do you want your mum for?" said James.
"I thought you were a big boy," said Harriet.

"Nearly,"
said Simon...

"...but not quite!"

Hallo! How Are You?

Shigeo Watanabe and Yasuo Ohtomo

"Hallo, flowers.
How are you?"

"Hallo, sparrows.
How are you?"

"Hallo, cat.
How are you?"

44

"Hallo, dog.
How are you?"

"Hallo, Mr Milkman.
How are you?"

"Hallo, Mr Paperman.
How are you?"

"Hallo, Mr Postman.
How are you?"

45

"Hallo, Mama.
How are you?"

"What a funny little bear you are."

"Wait. Wait!"

"Hallo, Papa.
How are you?"

"Hallo, Little Bear.
I'm very well,
thank you.
How are you?"

ANYONE SEEN HARRY LATELY?

Hiawyn Oram and Tony Ross

Whenever Harry did not like the way things looked, he disappeared...

re-appearing as some other Harry, for Harrysaurs are not required to tidy rooms or hang up clothes,

Harrylions are never
left with babysitters
half the night,

and Harryfish
are free to swim
and never told
to wash their ears
because they
have none.

49

So while others fought their battles face to face Harry sailed behind some great disguises and got away unscratched.

He thought, "Well, this is fun and this is peaceful," and started doing it all the time and couldn't stop himself

and then
forgot himself.

His mother was
the first to notice.
"Anyone seen
Harry lately?
I went to tuck
him up in bed
and found a
Harrygator."

His father went next door
to ask, "Anyone seen Harry
lately?"
The neighbours scratched
their heads and hummed,
"A Harrybat was here
last night - but Harry -
not for ages."

His friends came round
and rang the bell.

His mother, pale and cross, peered out, "Any of you seen
Harry lately?"
A Harrytank zoomed down the stairs and through the door
and up the street.
His friends said, "Nice - but that's not him.
We've not seen Harry lately."

52

He sat unfed.
(No one feeds strange
Harrystricters.)

He lay unkissed
(no one kisses
Harrybeetles) and
wondered where
he'd lost himself
along the road to
peace and quiet.

"I'd better have a search," he said
and called up all the characters
he'd used to wriggle out of things

and made them line up round the room
and stand there, marking time, all night.

But though he studied
carefully he couldn't
see himself at all.
Or wait a minute...
what was that...

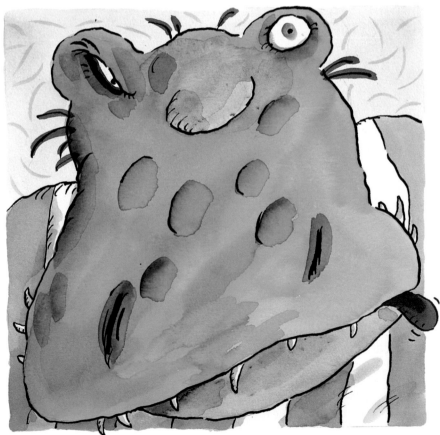

the sudden
narrowing of eyes...
the rudest little
tongue pulled out.
"Ah ha," he said,
"this looks like me..."
and urged his
characters to worse.

"Go on. Let's see. Get more like me.
Refuse to do what you are told,
to be the things you're
made to be."

Well, taking Harry at his word
and taking everything they'd need
those Harrycharacters made off
to find their own identity.

Still, good does
come of bad, because
a Harry stripped of all disguises
quickly re-materialises.

"Yoo hoo," he yelled
and ran into his
parents' room.
"Great news! Wake up!
I'm back! It's me!"
His parents rolled and
turned and stared.

"Who? Oh you!
Have you tidied up
your room?"
"Not yet," groaned
Harry, "maybe later.
Besides it wasn't me
who messed it.
I think it was that
Harrygator."

58

"It really is our Harry back," his parents sighed and let him in and held him tight in case he disappeared again

but Harry said, "No chance of that. Well, not tonight at any rate!"

IS THAT WHAT FRIENDS DO?

Marjorie Newman and Peter Bowman

Elephant sat gloomily on the river bank.
  Monkey came dancing along.
  "Hello, Elephant!" cried
Monkey. "All alone?"
  "Yes," sighed Elephant.
  "So am I!" said
Monkey. "Let's
be friends!"

  "I've never had a friend before," said Elephant.
  "I have. Lots!" cried Monkey.
"Why don't you come
and stay with me?"

"Is that what friends do?"
asked Elephant.

"Of course!" cried Monkey.

Monkey's doorway was too small for Elephant.

"Ow!" cried Elephant.

"Eee!" cried Elephant.

"Ah!" cried Elephant.

"I nearly got stuck."

"You are funny," cried Monkey, doubling up laughing, and not trying to help Elephant, *at all*.

Monkey switched on the radio.

The music was very loud.

"Let's dance!" cried Monkey.

"Is that what friends do?" asked Elephant.

"Of course!" cried Monkey. "Come on."

"Ow!" cried Elephant.
   "Eee!" cried Elephant.
   "Ah!" cried Elephant.
"I can't dance."

"You are funny," cried Monkey, spinning round on one leg, and
not trying to help Elephant, *at all*.

"We'll have scrambled eggs on toast for supper," said Monkey.

"I don't like scrambled eggs on toast," said Elephant.

"I do!" cried Monkey. "I'll let you be cook and we'll eat supper together."

"Is that what friends do?" asked Elephant.

"Of course!" cried Monkey.

"Ah!" cried Elephant.

"Eee!" cried Elephant.

"Ow!" cried Elephant. "I can't cook."

"You are funny!" laughed Monkey, sitting up at the table, and not trying to help Elephant, *at all*.

"Bedtime," announced Monkey. "Stay the night and you can sleep in my chair."

"Is that what friends do?" asked Elephant, trying to make himself comfortable.

"Of course," yawned Monkey.

"Ow!"
cried Elephant.
"Eee!" cried Elephant.
"Ah!" cried Elephant. "I'm falling off."

Monkey didn't even stir.
He slept very well.
He snored very loudly.

Elephant didn't sleep one wink. Not even with
cotton wool stuffed into his ears.

Next morning, Monkey woke up early.

"Come on, Elephant," he cried. "Let's go climbing."

"I don't like climbing, especially before breakfast," said Elephant.

"I do," cried Monkey. "We can climb together."

"Is that what friends do?" asked Elephant.

"Of course!" cried Monkey, putting on his jacket.

Elephant shivered outside the door.

"Hurry up, Elephant!" called Monkey. "We can climb this tree."

"Is that what friends do?" asked Elephant.

"Of course!" cried Monkey, already shinning high into the branches.

Elephant started to climb.
Crack went the branch.
Crash went Elephant.
"Ahhhhhhhhhh!" cried Elephant.

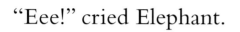

"Eee!" cried Elephant.

"Ow!" cried Elephant.

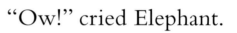

"I can't climb."

Monkey slid down the tree.
"Ah," said Monkey.
"Eee," said Monkey.
"Oh dear," said Monkey,
looking into a big
hole, and not
being able to see
Elephant, *at all*.

Monkey was all alone.

Further along the bank, Elephant sat gloomily. All alone.
  Monkey came walking by.
  "Oh, there you are,
Elephant," cried
  Monkey.

"Go away!"
growled Elephant.

Monkey was very quiet.
"Elephant," he said, "you
know I said I'd had lots
of friends?"

"Yes,"
sighed
Elephant.

"Well," said Monkey, "none of them stayed friends for long."
Elephant was quiet. Monkey was quiet. They were thinking.

"Elephant," said Monkey, after a while, "perhaps I got it all wrong."

"Oh?" said Elephant.

"Elephant," said Monkey. "Perhaps friends are kind to each other and share things."

"Oh!" said Elephant.

"Elephant," said Monkey. "Shall we try again?"

"Is that what friends do?" asked Elephant.

"Of course!" cried Monkey.

And they gave each other a great, big hug.

Mr Bill and Clarence
Kay Gallwey

Mr Bill is a kitten with a smart ginger moustache and long whiskers.
His fur is ginger and white.
He has big green eyes and because he is a Manx kitten, he has only a short stumpy tail.
On the night Mr Bill arrived he was tucked into a box with teddy and a cosy cover.

But next morning, Mr Bill wasn't with teddy in the box, or on the chair, or on the sofa, he was with Clarence in his big basket.

Clarence is a big Collie dog, with a long
golden coat, big white ruff, soft dark ears
and big brown eyes.

Mr Bill loves him.

Mr Bill
and Clarence
have breakfast
together.

Mr Bill tries a bit of Clarence's lunch. Clarence doesn't mind a bit.
They share a juicy bone for tea.

Mr Bill and Clarence
love to play together.

They play jumping the sofa.

They play hide and seek.

Mr Bill loves to jump out
and surprise Clarence.

76

Mr Bill hasn't got
a tail to play with,
so he borrows
Clarence's.

Mr Bill grows and grows.

But he still borrows
Clarence's tail.

Clarence wants to
borrow Mr Bill's
cat door, but he
is too big.

Every night, Mr Bill
washes himself,

then he washes
Clarence.

Then they curl
up together in
their big basket,
and go to sleep.
It's a bit of a
squash, but they
don't mind a bit.

RUBY
Maggie Glen

Ruby felt different from other bears - sort of special.

Mrs Harris had been day-dreaming when she made Ruby.
She didn't notice that she'd used the spotted material that was
meant for the toy leopards. She didn't watch carefully when she
sewed on the nose.

Ruby wasn't surprised when she was chosen from the other bears, but she didn't like being picked up by her ear.

"OUCH, GET OFF!" she growled.

Ruby's paw was stamped with an 'S' and she was thrown into the air.

"YIPEE-E-E-E! 'S' IS FOR SPECIAL," yelled Ruby.

Ruby flew across the factory and landed in a box full of bears.

"Hello," she said. "My name's Ruby and I'm special – see."

She held up her paw.

"No silly," laughed a big bear. "'S' is for second – second best."

"We're mistakes," said the bear with rabbit ears. "When the box is full, we'll be thrown out."

Ruby's fur stood on end; she was horrified.

More bears joined them in the box.

   At last the machines stopped.

   They listened to the workers as they chatted and hurried to catch the bus home.

   They heard the key turn in the lock.

   Then everything was quiet.

   One by one the bears fell asleep.

   All except Ruby – Ruby was thinking.

   The only sound was the sound of the big bear snoring.

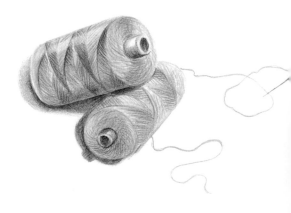

82

Hours passed. Suddenly Ruby shouted, "That's it!"

"What's it?" gasped the rabbit-eared bear
who woke up with a fright.

"Zzzzzzzzzzzzzzzzz-w-w-what's
going on?" groaned the big bear,
rubbing his sleepy eyes.

"That's *it*," said Ruby again. "We'll escape."

"ESCAPE!" they all shouted.
And they jumped out of the box.

"Let's go!" said Ruby.

83

They looked for a way out.
   They rattled the windows.
   They pushed at the doors.
   "There *is* no way out,"
cried a little bear.
"We're trapped."

"This way," shouted Ruby, rushing into the cloakroom.

They found a
broken air vent.
It was a very
tight squeeze.

They pushed and they pulled, they wiggled and they waggled, until
they were all in the yard outside.

They ran silently, swiftly, through the night and into the day.
Some ran to the country, some to the town.

Some squeezed
through letterboxes.

Some slipped through open windows.

Some hid in toy cupboards. Some crept into bed with lonely children.
But Ruby climbed into the window of the very best toy shop in town.

The other toys stared at Ruby.

"What's the 'S' for?" squealed the pigs.

"Special," said Ruby, proudly.

All the toys shrieked with laughter.

"Scruffy," said the smart-looking penguin.

"Soppy," said the chimpanzee.

"Stupid," giggled the mice.

"Very strange for a bear," they all agreed.

"Don't come next to me," said a prim doll.

"Wouldn't want to," said Ruby.

"Stand at the back," shouted the other toys.

They poked, they pulled, they prodded and they pinched. Ruby
pushed back as hard as she could, but there were too many of them.

So Ruby spent all day at the back of the shelf.

Then, just before closing time, a small girl came into the shop
with her grandfather.

They searched and searched for something –
something different, something special.

"That's the one," said the little girl.

"Yes, Susie,"
said Grandfather,
"that one looks
very special."

Ruby looked
around her. "Can
they see me?"

"IT'S ME! They're pointing at me. WHOOPEE-E-E-E!"

"We'll have that one, please," said Grandfather.

The shopkeeper put Ruby on the counter.

She looked at the 'S' on Ruby's paw.

"I'm sorry, sir," she said, "this one is a second. I'll fetch another."

"No thank you, that one is just perfect," said Grandfather. "It has character."

Character, thought Ruby, that sounds good.

"Shall I wrap it for you?" the shopkeeper asked.

"Not likely," growled Ruby. "Who wants to be shoved in a paper bag?"

"No thank you," said Susie. "I'll have her just as she is."

They all went out of the shop and down the street.

When they came to a yellow door they stopped.

"We're home, Spotty," said Susie.

"SPOTTY, WHAT A CHEEK!" muttered Ruby.

"It's got a growl," said Susie, and she and her grandfather laughed.

Susie took off her coat and scarf and sat Ruby on her lap.

Susie stared at Ruby and Ruby stared back.

Suddenly, Ruby saw a little silver 'S'
hanging on a chain round Susie's neck.

Hooray! thought Ruby.

One of us – a special.

ALL THE WAY TO THE STARS

Annalena McAfee and Anthony Lewis

I've had a lot of birthdays,
I even go to school.
I ride my bike all
    on my own,

and like to help around
the house.

But every day
my mummy says,
"Don't do that!
That's for big boys!"

When I'm big...

I'll climb to the top of the tower and stay up
all night to hear the owls hoot.

I'll eat all the sweets in the sweetshop

and ride a really huge bike.

When I'm a big boy I'll teach my teacher, and send my mummy to bed early for being naughty.

I'll drive a big red bus to the seaside,

go on every ride at the funfair, and no-one will ever say, "Don't do that! That's for big boys!"

I'll visit the zoo and join the monkeys for tea.
I'll have a pet pig and take him for walks in the woods.

When I'm a big boy,
I'll sail a ship to the top
and bottom of the world
to see the koalas in Australia,

the tigers in India,

the bears in Alaska, and the penguins in Antarctica.

and keep a parrot
that sings rude songs.

When I'm a big boy
I'll fly a plane all the
way to the stars. And
make sandcastles on
the moon.

I'll find heaps of buried treasure
when I'm a big boy,
and fight off silly pirates,

98

But I'll still come home to play with my toys

and see my mummy.

NANA'S GARDEN

Sophy Williams

One day in early autumn,
Thomas was going out to play.

"You come too, Nana,"
he said.

"Me?" said Nana. "I'm too
old to play."

"I wish you weren't," said
Thomas.

The sun cast shadows in Nana's garden. Thomas kicked up the leaves, still wet from the morning's rain. A branch cracked, an apple fell.

"Who's there?" said Thomas. The wind in the trees murmured, *"It's only me. An echo, a whisper, a heartbeat."*

The air grew cold in Nana's garden. Thomas turned and looked around. The long grass was flattened as if someone had been walking there. A trail of footsteps seemed to run in and out of the trees. Thomas followed them, all round the orchard and across the lawn to Nana's shed.

Thomas had never been inside, but now he thought perhaps there was something precious hidden there.

As he reached up to open the door, he thought he saw someone watching him.

"Who's there?" he said.

The wind whistled under the door. *"Inside,"* it said. *"Inside."*

A pale light shone through the little window, and lit up the muddle inside. Thomas began to search. Through the ancient chest of drawers, behind an old mirror, inside a box of rusty tools.

Then at the back of the shed Thomas found a tall cupboard. He opened the door. Dust flew up in a cloud. Spiders and mice scuttled. From a dark corner, a worn, friendly face looked out at him.

Very gently, very carefully, Thomas lifted out the treasure.

At the window, the small fingers of another child gripped the sill. There was a shimmer of blue, a wisp of hair, a bright eye watching.

"There, there," sang the other child. *"He's been waiting, all these long years."*

Thomas hugged the treasure and took it outside. As he sat on the damp grass he felt a tap on his shoulder.

"*Hello.*"

"Hello," said Thomas. "Who are you? This is Nana's garden."

"*It's my garden too,*" said the other child. "*I've come for Joshua.*"

"But I found him," said Thomas.

"*I know,*" she said. "*But he's mine.*"

The wind was very still. Thomas looked at the little girl.

"Let's play," he said.

They played with Joshua.

They played I-spy and giant's footsteps. They played statues and hide-and-seek. The sun came out. They raced in and out the trees – all around the orchard and up the steps.

 "Come on," said the other child. *"I'll show you the secret places."*

They ran through Nana's garden to the wild part where Thomas had never been before. Brambles caught at their clothes, leaves crunched under their feet.

"Look Thomas," said the other child. *"This is where Josie and Tsar are buried. Josie was a big sad labrador. Tsar was a snappy little terrier. He pined for days when Josie died. He didn't last long after."*

"And see that rose over there," said the child. *"I planted it because my name is Rose."*

"Nana's name is Rose too," said Thomas.

The light began to fade in Nana's garden.
   "I'm tired now," said Rose. *"I've got to go."*
   "Don't go," said Thomas. "Stay with me."
   "I am with you," she said. *"I'm always with you."*
   "Please don't go," said Thomas again.

110

But Rose was already through
the gate. Thomas ran after her.
"Here, take Joshua," he said.
"He's yours."

Then the light was gone in Nana's garden. There was no one there.
Just an echo, a shadow, a heartbeat.
Thomas ran back inside and hugged his grandmother fiercely.
  "I love you, Nana," he said.

FROG IN LOVE
Max Velthuijs

Frog was sitting on the river bank.
He felt funny.
He didn't know if he was happy or sad.
He had been walking about in a dream all week.
What could be wrong with him?

Then he met Piglet.
"Hello, Frog," said Piglet. "You don't look
very well. What's the matter with you?"
"I don't know," said Frog. "I feel like
laughing and crying at the same time.
And there's something going thump-thump
inside me, here."
"Maybe you've caught a cold," said Piglet.
"You'd better go home to bed."
Frog went on his way. He was worried.

115

Then he passed
Hare's house.
"Hare," he said,
"I don't feel well."
"Come along in and
sit down," said Hare,
kindly.
"Now then," said
Hare, "what's the
matter with you?"
"Sometimes I go hot,
and sometimes I go
cold," said Frog, "and

there's something going thump-thump inside me, here."
And he put his hand on his chest.
Hare thought hard, just like a real doctor.
"I see," he said. "It's your heart. Mine goes thump-thump too."

"But mine sometimes
thumps faster than usual,"
said Frog. "It goes one-two,
one-two, one-two."
Hare took a big book down
from his bookshelf and
turned the pages.
"Aha!" he said. "Listen to
this. Heartbeat, speeded up,
hot and cold turns...
it means you're in love!"
"In love?" said Frog, surprised. "Wow, I'm in love!"

And he was so pleased that
he did a tremendous jump
right out of the door and
up in the air.

Piglet was quite scared when Frog suddenly came falling from the sky. "You seem to be better," said Piglet. "I am! I feel just fine," said Frog. "I'm in love!" "Well, that's good news. Who are you in love with?" asked Piglet.

Frog hadn't stopped to think about that.

"I know!" he said. "I'm in love with the pretty, nice, lovely white duck!"

"You can't be," said Piglet. "A frog can't be in love with a duck. You're green and she's white."

But Frog didn't let that bother him. He couldn't write, but he could do beautiful paintings. Back at home he painted a lovely picture, with red and blue in it and lots of green, his favourite colour.

In the evening, when it was dark, he went out with his picture and pushed it under the door of Duck's house. His heart was beating hard with excitement.

Duck was very surprised when she found the picture. "Who can have sent me this beautiful picture?" she cried, and she hung it on the wall.

Next day Frog picked a beautiful bunch of flowers. He was going to give them to Duck. But when he reached her door, he felt too shy to face her. He put the flowers down on the doorstep and ran away as fast as he could go.

And so it went on, day after day. Frog just couldn't pluck up the courage to speak. Duck was very pleased with all her lovely presents. But who could be sending them?

Poor Frog! He didn't enjoy his food any more, and he couldn't sleep at night. Things went on like this for weeks. How could he show Duck he loved her?

"I must do something nobody else can do," he decided. "I must break the world high jump record! Dear Duck will be very surprised, and then she'll love me back."

121

Frog started training at once. He practised the high jump for days on end. He jumped higher and higher, right up to the clouds. No frog in the world had ever jumped so high before.

"What can be the matter with Frog?" asked Duck, worried. "Jumping like that is dangerous. He'll do himself an injury." She was right.

At thirteen minutes past two on Friday afternoon, things went wrong. Frog was doing the highest jump in history when he lost his balance and fell to the ground.

Duck, who happened to be passing at the time, came hurrying up to help him. Frog could hardly walk. Supporting him carefully, she took him home with her. She nursed him with tender loving care.

"Oh, Frog, you might have been killed!" she said. "You really must be careful. I'm so fond of you!"

And then, at last, Frog plucked up his courage. "I'm very fond of you too, dear Duck," he stammered. His heart was going thump-thump faster than ever, and his face turned deep green.

Ever since then, they have loved each other dearly.
A frog and a duck...
Green and white.
Love knows no boundaries.

Acknowledgements

THE PUBLISHERS GRATEFULLY ACKNOWLEDGE PERMISSION TO REPRODUCE THE
FOLLOWING STORIES, WHICH ARE PUBLISHED IN LONGER, COMPLETE EDITIONS
BY ANDERSEN PRESS:

Too Many Teddies © Gus Clarke 1995

Anyone Seen Harry Lately? Text © Hiawyn Oram 1988, Illustrations © Tony Ross 1988

Frog in Love © Max Velthuijs 1989

THE PUBLISHERS GRATEFULLY ACKNOWLEDGE AUTHORS AND ILLUSTRATORS
OF BOOKS PUBLISHED UNDER THEIR OWN IMPRINTS AS FOLLOWS:

Walking Round the Garden, published by The Bodley Head,
© John Prater 1998

An Evening at Alfie's, published by The Bodley Head,
© Shirley Hughes 1984

Nearly But Not Quite, published by The Bodley Head,
Text © Paul Rogers 1997, Illustrations © John Prater 1997

Hallo! How Are You?, published by The Bodley Head,
Text © Shigeo Watanabe 1979, English text © The Bodley Head 1980,
Illustrations © Yasuo Ohtomo 1979

Is That What Friends Do?, published by Hutchinson Children's Books,
Text © Marjorie Newman 1998, Illustrations © Peter Bowman 1998

Mr Bill and Clarence, published by The Bodley Head,
© Kay Gallwey 1990

Ruby, published by Hutchinson Children's Books,
© Maggie Glen 1990

All the Way to the Stars, published by Julia MacRae Books,
Text © Annalena McAfee 1995, Illustrations © Anthony Lewis 1995

Nana's Garden, published by Hutchinson Children's Books,
© Sophy Williams 1993